GIRLS CAUSIN' CHAOS

To my Pompom dad

Ö CONTENTS Ö

← Scan the QR Code

Find an Easter egg

02

The End

NORTH POLE MADNESS

Lonny

Hailey

Gravety

Home Sweet Home

12

13

The End

THE KITTY SQUAD

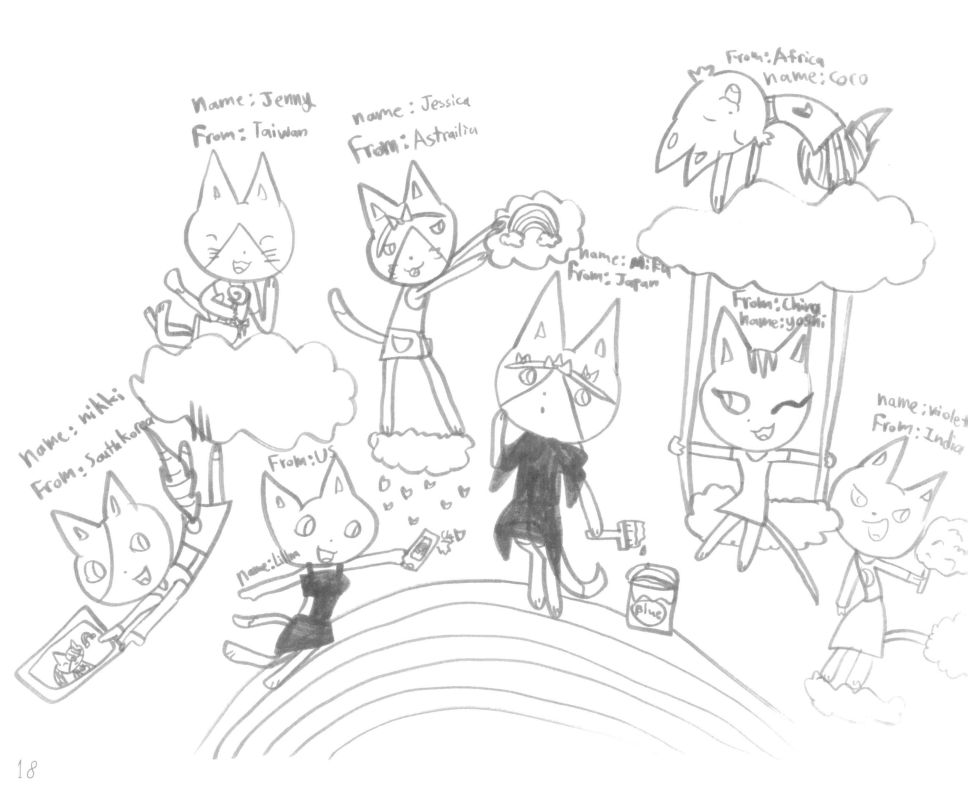

Name: Jenny
From: Taiwan

name: Jessica
From: Astrailia

From: Africa
name: Coco

Name: Mifu
From: Japan

From: China
name: yoshi

Name: nikki
From: South korea

From: US

Name: Lillian

name: violet
From: India

Blue

18

name : Miku

hickname : (Miku had
no hickname, it's Miku.)

From : Japan

Miku

Nikki

Name: Nikki
nickname: Nik
From: South korea

21

Lillna

name: Lillna

nickname: Lilly

From: U.S (United States)

Yoshi

name: Yoshi
nickname: Yosh
From: China

Jessica

name: Jessica
Nickname: Sasha
From: Australia

Violet

name: Violet
hickname: vio
From: India

Curry salt

Jenny

name: Jenny
nick name: Jen
From: Taiwan

Coco

name : coco
hickname: coke
From : Africa
Age : 7

This is Stella

30

34

This is Stella's
bedroon

We Played with Mena for 10 Weeks until Stella's birthday!

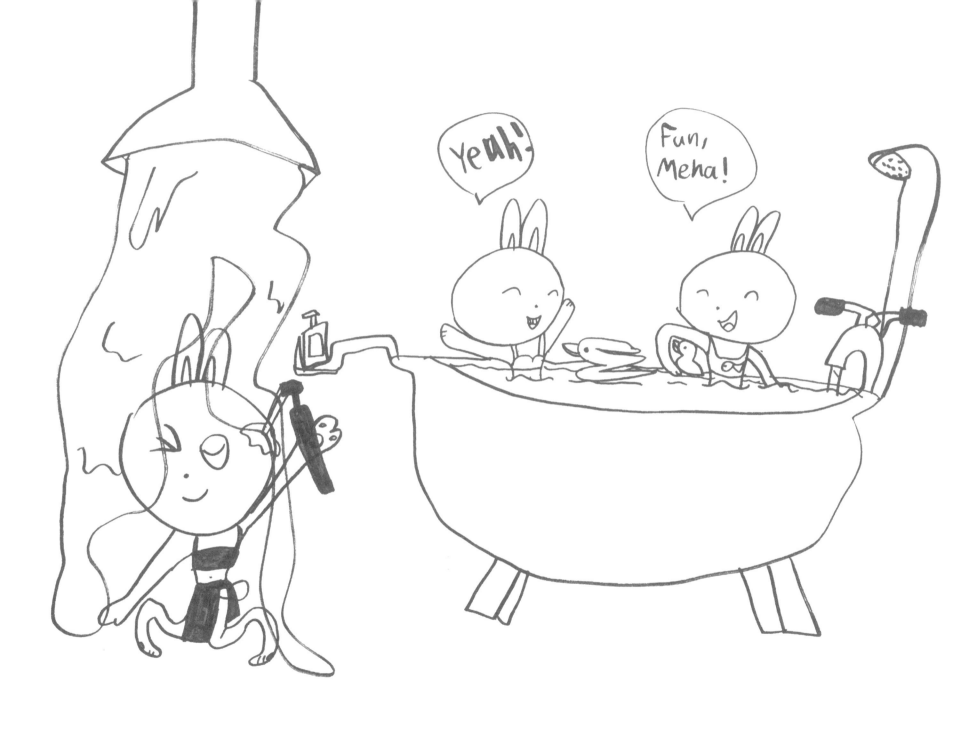

42

44

School DAY worries! Weekends fun!

zoom!

School day

AHH!! I forgot to pack my backpack, yesterday!

47

48

School day

49

50

GIRLS CAUSIN' CHAOS

Printed in Taiwan, Republic of China

For information address:

Elephant White Cultural Enterprise Ltd. Press,

8F.-2, No.1, Keji Rd., Dali Dist., Taichung City 41264, Taiwan (R.O.C.)

Distributed by Elephant White Cultural Enterprise Co., Ltd.

ISBN: 978-626-7189-92-4

Suggested Price: NT$ 777